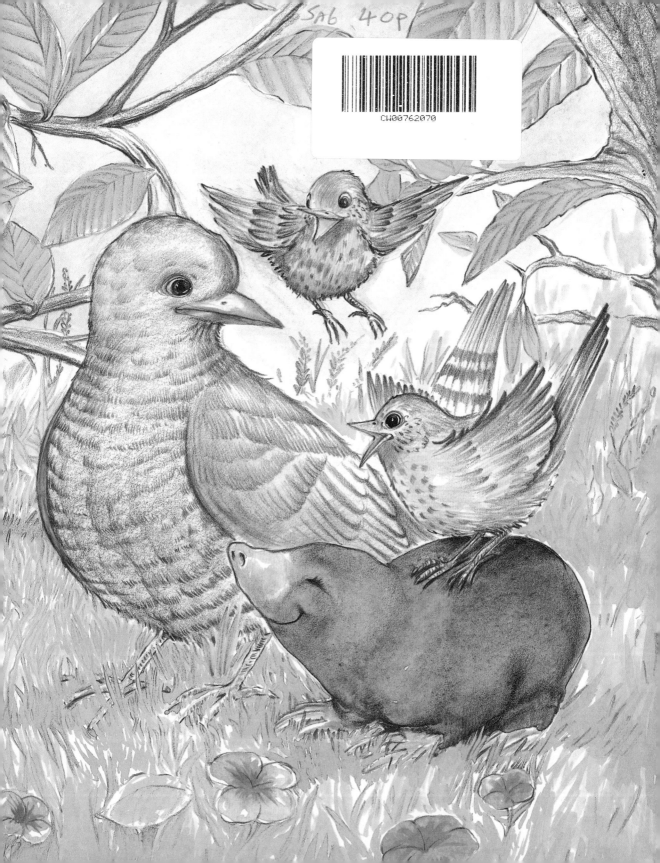

ISBN 1 85854 529 3
© Brimax Books Ltd 1997. All rights reserved.
Published by Brimax Books Ltd, Newmarket,
England, CB8 7AU 1997.
Printed in China.

Woodland Stories

by Fiona Hurlock

Illustrated by Pauline Hazelwood

Brimax · Newmarket · England

A Cuckoo in the Nest

Tilly and Tommy Thrush are very proud. They are looking after the most beautiful, perfect, little speckled egg you have ever seen. Just one. Sometimes they sit together and gaze proudly at the egg, looking forward to when their chick will hatch. One day, Tilly and Tommy both have something important to do. They both leave the nest with its tiny egg just for a very few moments.

While they are out, someone comes to visit them. It is Mrs Cuckoo. "Cuckoo! Tilly and Tommy!" she calls. "Is there anyone at home? Cuckoo!" When no-one answers Mrs Cuckoo does something rather strange. She slides onto Tilly's nest and quickly lays an egg of her own. It is bigger than Tilly's and not nearly as beautiful. Then she flies away.

Tilly is in such a hurry to get back to the nest that she flies down and sits on it straight away. She hasn't noticed that there are now two eggs. Soon afterwards she feels some tiny movements in the nest. Tommy can hear funny little crunching, cracking noises. It is the egg. They both jump up and there, looking up at them, are two feathery little heads with great big eyes.

"We've got twins!" cries Tilly.

Tilly and Tommy decide to call their new babies Tony and Tiny Thrush. Tony looks exactly like his mother and father. Tiny, on the other hand, does not. He looks completely different. His name does not suit him very well either. Although he is called Tiny, he isn't tiny at all. In fact, he is huge! Tiny is the biggest baby thrush anyone has ever seen. He is also the hungriest!

When Tony eats a worm, Tiny eats three worms! When Tony munches a berry, Tiny munches five berries! Very soon Tiny grows to be as big as Tilly and Tommy. Then, he grows some more. Soon he grows too big for the nest and has to live on the branch just outside. He loves his mother and father and his little brother so he doesn't really mind.

Tommy teaches Tony and Tiny to fly. Tiny goes first and does very well. Tony has a go and falls straight to the ground. With Tiny's help he soon gets the hang of it. Next Tilly teaches them to sing. Tony goes first. He is good at singing. He has a beautiful voice. Then Tiny has a go. He can't manage the same pretty song as Tony. He makes a very strange noise that sounds a bit like "Cuckoo!"

Mrs Cuckoo hears Tiny's strange singing from far in the distance. She flies off to find the nest. As she flies towards it she flies straight into Tony! (He is still practising his flying). "Cuckoo! Look out!" she shouts, but it is too late. CRASH! "Oh Tiny!" says Tony. "Do look where you are going!" When Tony looks up, he realises that it isn't Tiny who has crashed into him at all. It is someone else who looks just like him.

Tilly, Tommy and Tiny hear the crash and come to see what has happened. When they see Mrs Cuckoo they stare at her in amazement. "You look exactly like Tiny...only even bigger!" says Tommy. "You sound exactly like Tiny...only even louder!" says Tilly. Mrs Cuckoo looks back at them and laughs. "Of course we look and sound alike," she says. "All cuckoos are like this."

Tiny looks closely at Mrs Cuckoo and then at Tilly and Tommy. Suddenly he understands everything. He has often wondered why he is so different from the others in his family. He thinks for a moment.

"Well," he says. "I may look like a cuckoo. I may sound like a cuckoo. But my name is Tiny Thrush. This is my family and this is my home. This is where I shall stay!"

Can you find five differences between these two pictures?

Can you say these words and tell the story by yourself?

egg

Tiny

Tony

Mrs Cuckoo

Mole sees the Light

At the edge of a big wood, just across the pond, there lives a mole called Molly. Molly is an ordinary mole in almost every way. She lives in the dark in a cosy burrow under the ground and makes tunnels whenever she wants to go anywhere - just like all the other moles.

And just like all the other moles, Molly sleeps during the day when the sun is up and is awake at night, after the sun has gone to bed.

But Molly is different from other moles. Even though she lives underground in the dark and she comes out at night when it is dark, she does not like the dark. She hates it. Poor Molly is very unhappy.

Molly wants to change her life so that she doesn't have to live in the dark anymore.
When all the other moles have gone to bed for a long day's sleep, Molly tries to stay awake.
When all the other moles wake up, Molly goes to bed but she can't sleep because of the noise.
The other moles are tunnelling and keeping her awake with their digging.

Molly tries going outside during the day to be in the sunshine but she finds that the bright light hurts her eyes. She tries sunglasses but they don't help. Poor Molly has to keep her eyes closed in the bright sunshine. It is just like being in the dark again.

Molly thinks she should try and find a new place to live instead of the dark burrow with the other moles. Her friends, Squirrel, Woodpecker, and Owl, all live in a tree nearby and Molly decides to try and find a home there also. But poor Molly cannot climb up the tree like the squirrel; she cannot peck a hole like the woodpecker; and she cannot fly into the branches like the owl.

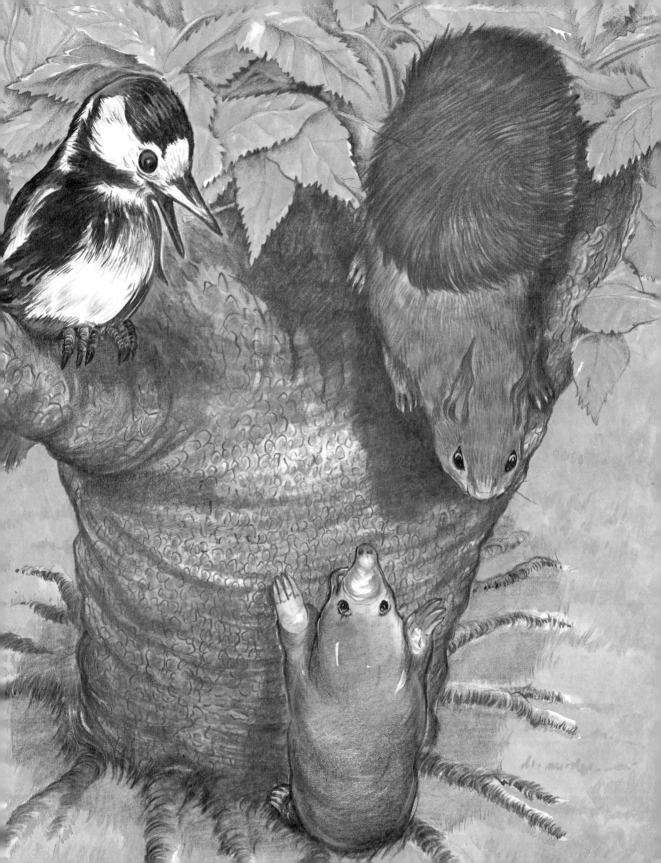

Oh dear! Poor Molly! None of her ideas have worked. What can she do?

"I'll ask Owl. He is very wise," she thinks. "He will know what I should do." Off she goes to find him.

When Molly finds Owl she tells him her troubles. "I am not like the other moles," she explains. "I live underground in the dark like they do. I am awake at night when it is dark like they are. I live my whole life in the dark like they do. The problem is . . . I hate the dark!"

Owl looks surprised by this sad story. This is the first time he has met a mole who doesn't like the dark and he wants to find out more. "Tell me Molly," says Owl. "Do you know why you do not like the dark. Are you afraid of the dark?"

"Of course not," says Molly. "I simply don't like it because I can't see very well and I keep bumping into everything."

When Owl hears this he laughs. "But Molly," he says. "It's not because it's dark that you can't see very well. It's because your eyes are not very strong. All you need is a pair of glasses."
Molly is delighted that Owl has solved her problem so easily.
If only she had come to see him in the first place. Molly and Owl laugh together. At last, Molly has seen the light.

Can you find five differences between these two pictures?

Can you say these words and tell the story by yourself?

Squirrel

Woodpecker

Molly

Owl

Squirrel's New Home

In a big tree, near the edge of a medium-sized wood, lives a small squirrel. Squirrel has a nice home in the tree. It is comfortable and cosy. All around Squirrel's tree are other trees. Squirrel's tree has big green leaves. All the other trees have big green leaves too.

Squirrel likes to sit in his tree and look out at the world. He can see trees and more trees. He can see green leaves and more green leaves. In fact, all Squirrel can see from his tree are other trees. All he can see are trees with hundreds and thousands of green leaves.

One day Squirrel realises that he
is fed up with green.
Green is boring.
Green is dull.
Green is tiresome.
Green is green.
Green is everywhere!

There are big green leaves and small green leaves. There are dark green leaves and light green leaves.
Some leaves are shiny.
Some leaves are smooth.
Some leaves are spiky.
Some leaves are furry.
But they are all green!

Squirrel sees a bird and says, "Excuse me. Do you know the way to the seaside? I want a new home. If I can find a tree near the seaside, I can look out at the beach with bright yellow sand and red umbrellas. I can also look out at the blue sea."

"Of course I know the way," says the bird. "That's where I'm going now as the winter is coming. It's much too far for a squirrel. You'll have to stay here in the wood."

Poor Squirrel is sad. Imagine waking up to all those beautiful bright things to look at. What a lovely change it would make from green, green, green! Squirrel goes to bed and when, at last, he falls asleep, he dreams of all the wonderful places in the world where he would like to live. He dreams of a comfortable, cosy home in a tree with a rich and beautiful view.

When Squirrel wakes up the next morning, he wonders if he is still dreaming. He climbs out of bed, stretches, yawns and rubs his eyes. He cannot believe what he sees outside.

Yellow, gold and orange leaves have appeared on the trees. Everywhere Squirrel looks he sees beautiful, bright reds and warm browns. Squirrel has never seen anything so wonderful. He sits for a whole day in his tree watching the changes of the season all around him. Whenever a breeze blows, some of the leaves flutter away to the ground, making a carpet of gold, yellow, red and brown.

Squirrel looks all around him. Then he sees a little piece of the most beautiful blue. The clear, bright sky was peeping through the trees. "I do not need to move to the seaside," says Squirrel. "I have the most beautiful home in the world right here where I belong."

Can you find five differences between these two pictures?

Can you say these words and tell the story by yourself?

leaves

bird

umbrellas

branches

All
Winter Long

In a big tree, at the edge of a wood, there lives a small family of squirrels. Mr Squirrel has an enormous, bushy tail of which he is very proud. Mrs Squirrel is smaller. Her tail is just as bushy but not quite as long. They live with their son, Sam Squirrel.

One morning, the squirrels wake up to find that it is very, very cold. They look outside and see that something is different. Their tree no longer has any leaves on it. Not a single one. All the leaves have fallen to the ground or been blown away. Instead, on the branches, there are very small, sparkly, white crystals which glisten in the sunshine.

"Look Sam," says Mr Squirrel.
"That is frost. The frost means that
winter is coming. We must start to
get ready."
"Ready for what?" asks Sam.
"For the winter, of course," says
his father. "Now I must go and
warn your mother." Off he went.

Mr and Mrs Squirrel get straight to work. They fetch berries and acorns. They carry leaves, feathers and pieces of grass. Everything is taken inside. Sam doesn't help because he doesn't know what they are doing. When he goes inside to see what is going on, he sees that the cupboards are being filled with food and the beds are being piled high with cosy leaves, grass and feathers.

"What are you doing?" asks Sam. Mrs Squirrel explains. "Winter is coming. It will be very cold. The ground will be hard and there will be no food. We must stay inside to keep warm. We will curl up in our cosy beds and go to sleep. When we wake up, we will have all the food we need and we won't have to go outside until the spring."

Sam thinks this sounds like a very good idea. He doesn't like the cold one bit. What he loves to do most of all is spend the day curled up in bed eating acorns. "How long will we sleep for?" he asks his father.

"All winter long," is the reply. "When will we start?" asks Sam. "When winter comes," says his mother. "There is lots of work to be done if we are to be ready."

Sam Squirrel wakes up each
morning and looks out to see
if winter has come.
On some days it is warm.
On some days it is cold.
On some days it is wet.
On some days it is dry.
But he never sees the soft, white
snow on the ground to say that
winter has come.

One morning, Sam wakes to hear a robin singing on a branch outside. When he looks out he has to rub his eyes to make sure he isn't dreaming. The whole world is white. The trees are white and the ground is white.
Everything is white!
This is better than frost -
this is snow! This is winter!

"Winter is here! It has come at last!" shouts Sam. "It is time to curl up in our new, warm beds and wait for spring." Sam is so excited. He has been looking forward to snuggling down in the warm with his big pile of berries and nuts. It does seem a shame to miss the snow - it looks fun. "Perhaps the snow will be here in the spring," says Sam. "Maybe it will stay white all winter long!"

Can you find five differences between these two pictures?

Can you say these words and tell the story by yourself?

berries

acorns

feathers

leaves